green kids club

in India

jade elephant

Written by Sylvia M. Medina & Saige J. Ballock-Dixon

Illustrations by Joy Eagle

Consultants - Peggy Hinman, Noor H Faheem
and Ashley Perez

Green Kids Club Adventures
The Green Spring (First Story)
Ice Jams
Coral Reef
Jade Elephant

Published by Green Kids Club, Inc.
P.O. Box 50030
Idaho Falls, ID 83405

ISBN 978-0-9836602-4-8

Copyright ©2012 by Green Kids Club, Inc.
ALL RIGHTS RESERVED

*This book is dedicated to the children of India
and all the Green Kids of the world.*

Maya and Victor Green were sitting on the steps of a beautiful temple in India. Maya was twirling a jade elephant on a chain that her mother had given her. It was green and gold and glittered in the bright sunshine. The Green Kids were waiting for their friend Anju. Anju was going to show them the village in the forestlands of her beautiful country and the Green Kids were excited!

4

Just then Anju emerged from the forest riding a colorfully decorated Asian elephant. Close behind followed a smaller decorated elephant.

"Anju, over here!" Victor called. Victor and Maya looked at each other with excitement. They had never ridden an elephant before.

Maya walked up to the gentle giant, "Why is she wearing these fancy blankets and shiny ornaments?"

"We decorate her because she is special to our village," Anju said. "We depend on her to help us work and to take us places. Her name is Mudahrima and this is her baby, Gajendra. We call him baby Gaj." Baby Gaj stepped from behind his mother to greet the Green Kids.

"Hop on up and we will go to my village!" Anju called to Victor and Maya.

6

Mudahrima knelt down and the Green Kids climbed up. At first Victor and Maya were a little nervous. They were way, way above the ground, and Mudahrima's heavy steps rocked them from side to side.

They started through the forest on the path to the village. As they rode, Victor and Maya noticed that the forest was full of funny looking plants and strange noises that they had never seen or heard before. A peacock, the national bird of India, welcomed the children to the forest.

Anju began pointing out the turquoise kingfisher and yellow oriole flying through the air. They saw a red panda family playing in the orchids and an Asian fishing cat searching for his supper. They even caught a glimpse of a great Bengal tiger in the distance.

As the Green Kids got closer and closer to the village, they noticed the forest was not as thick. Trees had been cut down and the ground was bare.

"Anju, why are so many trees cut down?" Maya asked.

Anju explained, "My father and the other villagers are cutting the trees so we can grow more crops."

"Anju, we should talk to your father," Maya said, "He may not know it, but this could destroy the forest. If there is no forest, where will the animals live?"

Just then the children heard loud trumpeting noises.

"What is that?" Victor exclaimed, "That's the loudest sound I've ever heard!"

Anju replied, "Can't you tell what that is? It is the sound of elephants calling each other. It is coming from the elephant place."

"Elephant place?" Maya asked.

Anju explained, "It is the place where the elephant families gather together."

Anju knew she probably should not take the kids to see the elephant place. Still, Victor and Maya had come to see all the amazing mysteries of the Indian forests, so Anju decided to take them there.

Guided by Anju's gentle promptings, Mudahrima and baby Gaj turned and began walking slowly towards the trumpeting sounds. As they came closer to the elephant place, Anju told Mudahrima to stop before they would be noticed by the other elephants.

As the children peered from their hiding place, they saw elephants gathering around a pool of water. They were all looking and listening intently to the largest elephant who was talking to them. Anju quietly said to Victor and Maya, "That is the matriarch of the herd, Parmita."

Parmita was making an urgent speech to the herd, "We must destroy the village if we want to survive. The people there are cutting down our forest for their farmland. If we don't destroy the village, we will have no place to live and no food to eat." The herd nodded and grunted loudly in agreement.

Frightened by Parmita's strong words, baby Gaj let out a baby elephant squeal. All of the elephants immediately turned to the Green Kids' hiding place. Parmita was angry at the intrusion of the humans. Parmita ran over, and with her trunk she yanked Anju from Mudahrima's back and tossed her into the pool.

Anju was stunned, and as she went under the pool's surface, she accidentally took a large gulp of water. Immediately, Anju felt very strange. This pool was one of the world's magic springs — like the spring Victor and Maya had gained their power to speak with animals.

As she came back up to the surface, Anju heard Parmita say, "We need to get rid of these humans and destroy the village now. They know our plan."

"Please, please, listen to me Parmita!" Anju begged. "We can help you. Please do not hurt us or our village."

Victor and Maya jumped down from Mudahrima's back and came running over. "Yes, yes, we can help save your forest home! Please listen to us!"

"Let us go back and talk with Anju's father, who is the leader of the village," Maya said. "We can help him and the other villagers understand they are destroying your forest home. We can teach them ways to use the land better. They love the forest and all the animals in it. Surely they will understand and help to save your home."

Parmita agreed to let Anju and the Green Kids try, but was not sure it would work. She had seen too much destruction by humans in her lifetime.

"Go! But if the destruction of the forest does not stop, we will come and destroy your home in order to protect our own," Parmita said. "We have no other choice."

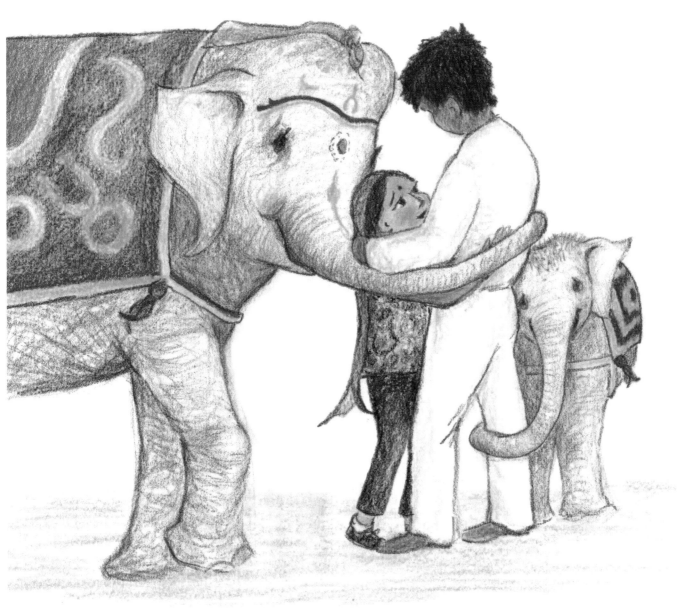

Anju, Victor and Maya jumped on Mudahrima and rode quickly away following the stern warning of Parmita.

As they entered the village, Anju saw her father and ran straight into his arms.

"Father, we must not destroy the forest lands any longer," she said. "The elephants are angry, and they will be coming to destroy our village if we do not stop."

"How do you know this?" Anju's father asked.

"Parmita warned us," Anju said. "We must share the land with the elephants. If not, they will destroy our village."

Just then Anju's father heard trumpeting coming from the forest in loud, short bursts. He raised his head toward the noise and listened.

Anju's father said, "This is a very difficult request you make of our village. We need the land for crops."

Victor spoke up, "We can teach you ways to use the land and how to plant your farms so that you will have more crops without having to destroy more forest."

Anju's father listened to Victor and Maya's ideas about how to plant their crops and liked what he heard.

23

Anju's father recognized the Green Kids' wisdom "Anju, Victor, Maya, you are right. I will share what I have learned with the whole village. Tell Parmita we will not destroy any more forest. Instead we will use the land we have carefully."

Anju turned to Mudahrima and smiled.

"Go and tell Parmita that we will change! We will not destroy any more of the forest," Anju said as she gazed into Mudahrima's eyes.

Anju could see that her own beautiful elephant friend was sad. As Anju looked into her dark eyes, she saw the forest lands and the reflection of other elephants. She then understood that her friend yearned to return to her home and family.

Anju knew in her heart what she must do. "My good friend and faithful partner," Anju whispered. "I will let you and baby Gaj go and be free."

The Green Kids removed the colorful blankets and ornaments from Mudahrima. Mudahrima bowed her head in one final show of respect. With tears in her eyes, Anju kissed Mudahrima and hugged baby Gaj one last time. Mudahrima reached out with her trunk and slowly caressed Anju's face. Anju took her hand and softly touched Mudahrima's trunk. Mudahrima and baby Gaj slowly turned away and started walking toward the other elephants.

"Thank you Green Kids for helping save our forest and our village!" Anju said, gesturing toward the elephants.

Soon they heard loud, joyous trumpeting coming from the forests. Mudahrima spread the word to Parmita and the other elephants.

"Thank you for saving our lands in this magical place!" they heard Parmita exclaiming. "The Green Kids are true friends to all who live here! Now we can go forward together in peace!"

These words made Anju happy. She hugged Victor and Maya and thanked them again. "I will miss Mudahrima, but she needs to be with her family."

Suddenly, Maya had an idea. She took the jade elephant and chain from her neck and placed it around Anju's neck. "Now you will have this jade elephant so you will always remember your friend Mudahrima and baby Gaj!"

29

With this, the Green Kids said farewell to Anju and started
down the path back to the temple and on to their next adventure.

asian elephants

© Can Stock Photo Inc. / shariffc

Asian elephants are smaller than the African elephant, but still weigh up to 11,000 lbs and measure up to 10 feet high. Females don't usually have visible tusks and not all males have them.

Female and young male elephants live in small family groups while mature males live alone or with other mature bulls. Elephants live to be about 60 years old in the wild.

The habitat of Asian elephants consists of broadleaf tropical forests, such as Southeast Asia.

© Can Stock Photo Inc. / joyfull

Elephants eat grasses, tree bark, roots, leaves and small stems. They also love bananas, rice and sugarcane crops. They eat about 150 lbs of food a day.

Elephant trunks are like human fingers. They use their trunks like arms and fingers to touch, grab and move things.

© Can Stock Photo Inc. / sandsphoto

© Can Stock Photo Inc. / FionaCunningham

Asian elephants have been used by humans for over 4,000 years. They have been used for harvesting crops, for travel and for religious ceremonies.

Asian elephants are often decorated with special paint, ornaments and cloth for ceremonies.

© Can Stock Photo Inc. / StrangerView

© Can Stock Photo Inc. / Clivia

how are asian elephants threatened?

Asian elephants are endangered.   As the number of people increase, the more land humans use and the less land there is for elephants.

The land is being converted from tropical forests full of food for the elephants to farmland, human living space and development, such as roads, dams and mines.

Due to the loss of habitat, elephants have been eating crops causing human-elephant conflict. The conflicts usually end with the elephants being killed.

how can humans help?

Humans can help protect the remaining elephants by conserving their habitat. Setting up conservation areas for elephants and other wildlife that will remain natural will save habitat for elephants.

Teaching people to use the most conservative practices for growing crops to reduce the amount of land needed for farming will help protect more land for elephants and other wild animals.

By using practices that keep elephants from damaging crops, conflicts with humans can be avoided. These practices can be barriers around crops or smells that elephants do not like.

CPSIA information can be obtained
at www.ICGtesting.com
Printed in the USA
272876LV00001B

9 780983 660248